FATAL BEAUTY

c.3

FATAL BEAUTY

Andre Holder

Illustrations by Jack Tom

NEW WRITERS' VOICES

Readers House

Literacy Volunteers of New York City

NEW WRITERS' VOICES ™ was made possible by grants from an anonymous foundation; Exxon Corporation; Scripps Howard Foundation; Philip Morris Companies, Inc.; Garry Trudeau and Penguin USA; and H. W. Wilson Foundation.

ATTENTION READERS: We would like to hear what you think about our books. Please send your comments or suggestions to:

The Editors, Readers House
Literacy Volunteers of New York City
121 Avenue of the Americas
New York, NY 10013

New Writers' Voices is a series of books published by Readers House, the publishing division of Literacy Volunteers of New York City, Inc., 121 Avenue of the Americas, New York, NY 10013. The words, "New Writers' Voices," are a trademark of Readers House/ Literacy Volunteers of New York City. READERS HOUSE and colophon are trademarks of Literacy Volunteers of New York City.

Cover designed by Paul Davis Studio.
Interior designed by AnneLouise Burns.
Illustrations by Jack Tom.

This book was edited with the cooperation and consent of the author.

Executive Director, LVNYC: Lilliam Barrios-Paoli
Publishing Director, LVNYC: Nancy McCord
Managing Editor: Sarah Kirshner
Publishing Coordinator: Yvette Martinez-Gonzalez
Marketing/ Production Manager: Elizabeth Bluemle

LVNYC is an affiliate of Literacy Volunteers of America.

ACKNOWLEDGMENTS

Literacy Volunteers of New York City gratefully acknowledges the generous support of the following foundations and corporations that made the publication of READERS HOUSE books possible: An anonymous foundation; Exxon Corporation; Scripps Howard Foundation; Philip Morris Companies, Inc.; Garry Trudeau and Penguin USA; and H. W. Wilson Foundation.

We deeply appreciate the contributions of the following suppliers: Cam Steel Rule Die Works Inc. (steel cutting die for display); Domtar Industries (text stock); Horizon Paper Company (cover stock); MCUSA (display header); Delta Corrugated Container (corrugated display); Offset Paperback Manufacturers, Inc., A Bertelsmann Company (cover and text printing and binding); and Phototype Color Graphics (cover color separations).

For their guidance, support and hard work, we are indebted to the LVNYC Board of Directors' Publishing Committee: James E. Galton, Marvel Comics Ltd.; Virginia Barber, Virginia Barber Literary Agency, Inc.; Doris Bass, Scholastic, Inc.; Jeff Brown; Jerry Butler; George P. Davidson, Ballantine Books; Joy M. Gannon, St. Martin's Press; Walter Kiechel,

Fortune; Geraldine E. Rhoads; Virginia Rice, Reader's Digest; Martin Singerman, News America Publishing, Inc.; James L. Stanko, James Money Management, Inc.; and Arnold Schaab and F. Robert Stein of Pryor, Cashman, Sherman & Flynn.

Thanks also to Joy Gannon and Claire Walsh of St. Martin's Press for producing this book; Gretchen Van Nuys for her editing and interviewing skills; Ed Susse for photography; and Lisa Holzer for her thoughtful copyediting and suggestions.

Our thanks to Paul Davis Studio and Myrna Davis, Paul Davis, Lisa Mazur, Hajime Ando, Haruetai Muodtong and Chalkley Calderwood for their inspired design of the covers of these books. Thanks also to AnneLouise Burns for her sensitive design of the interior of this book and to Jack Tom for his stylish illustrations.

The author would like to thank Pauline Clarke, Paul Schmitz, Lise Scott and Judy Sullivan.

CONTENTS

LOUIS PIERRE

ROY LONG

TRACY SULLIVAN

CAST OF CHARACTERS

LOUIS PIERRE, the narrator of the story. He is an insurance company detective who is originally from France. He is tall and well-built but dresses badly. He is a loner and lives only for his job. He has a "live and let die" attitude toward others.

ROY LONG, the owner of Long Life Insurance Company and Louis's boss. He is short, fat and bald. He is cheap and has a quick temper.

TRACY SULLIVAN, a recent widow who comes to Long Life Insurance to claim her husband's life insurance policy. She is tall, blonde and blue-eyed. Her pale skin has a rosy glow. Her voluptuous body contrasts with her innocent-looking face. She is every man's dream girl.

A SPECIAL ASSIGNMENT

I am a detective. I work for a firm called Long Life Insurance Company in New York City. My boss's name is Roy Long. I have worked for Mr. Long for ten years now.

It was the second day of January 1957. I woke up bright and early to go to work. Long Life Insurance is in a large office building downtown.

The detectives hang their hats in a large office on the main floor.

When I got there, Mr. Long called and told me to report to his office. He sounded upset. Mr. Long has a bad temper.

I paced while I waited for the elevator to go up to Mr. Long's office. When the elevator finally came, a beautiful blue-eyed blonde stepped out.

My heart skipped a beat. She was like a gift from heaven. I said, "Hello." She glanced at me and smiled but kept on walking.

On the elevator, I couldn't stop

thinking about her. I had never cared much about women before. I was married to my job.

Mr. Long looked mad as I sat down in front of his desk. He was short and fat and had a bald head. He said, "Louis, I have a special assignment for you. I think we might have a *black widow* kind of case. You know — like the spider who kills her mates.

"I just had a visit from a lady named Tracy Sullivan. Her second husband just died, naming her as the beneficiary of his life insurance policy worth 5.1 million dollars. He was the head of a Wall Street law firm.

"The police have called it a natural death, but I believe she killed him for the money. When her first husband died, I was suspicious. He too had a big life insurance policy with us. This time I'm sure something fishy is going on. I want you to get close to her and try to trap her."

"When would you like me to get started?" I asked.

"Right away, but you will need to change your image first. Tracy Sullivan likes men with money. You will need to impress her. We will get you a new identity. You will be an investment consultant and your name will be Jean-Claude Emmanuel."

Mr. Long showed me a picture of Tracy Sullivan. She was the beautiful blonde I had seen at the elevator. I was glad because now I knew I would see her again.

A NEW IMAGE

Over the next few weeks, I turned myself into the image of a rich man. I got a good haircut and went on a shopping spree. I said good-bye to my sixth-floor, walk-up apartment and moved into a spacious one on the fashionable Upper East Side of town. I started going to society functions, art galleries and popular clubs.

I didn't mind leaving my old life behind. What family I had was back in France, where I was raised. We weren't close. I had no friends to speak of. My job was my life.

A FATEFUL MEETING

I got lucky and found Tracy at my first black-tie party. I saw her as I walked in. She smiled at me. I knew she didn't recognize me because I looked different from that day we first saw each other. My tuxedo suited my slim, six-foot two-inch build, and my new hair stylist had done wonders with my thick hair.

We introduced ourselves. I was amazed by Tracy's beauty. She had an innocent-looking face and a voluptuous body with long, shapely legs. She was wearing a form-fitting, red evening dress and her matching shoes had stiletto heels.

I had never met anyone like her before. At that moment, I couldn't think about work. There were sparks between us. Tracy said, "Would you like to go for a walk?"

"I would like that very much," I said. As we left the party, I had a better idea. "Why don't we go for a drink? I know this little place downtown. My limousine is outside."

When we got to the bar, it was closed. I hadn't realized it was 2:15 in the morning. We stopped for a moment. Then Tracy said, "Would you like to have a drink at my place?"

"Why not? Where do you live?"

"Park Avenue."

When we got there, I saw that Tracy lived in the penthouse. It was beautiful. She said, "Would you like some champagne?"

"Champagne will be fine," I replied. We sat on the sofa and talked.

Tracy turned on some music.

Then she turned off the light and said, "Let's dance."

We danced in the dark. Tracy kissed me like I had never been kissed before. We danced toward the bedroom, Frank Sinatra's "Strangers in the Night" playing in the background.

Tracy kissed me from my toes up. She poured scented oil all over my body and massaged me. It was erotic, sensual and provocative.

The music stopped. The silence was broken only by the sound of our breathing. We didn't speak. We made love for five hours, something I had never done before.

As I got dressed and walked to the door, I could feel Tracy's desire pulling me back. She said, "Just give me a little more time. I'm not ready to let you go."

I couldn't help but go back to her. I was falling in love with the woman I was supposed to trap. I couldn't stop myself.

A BIG STEP

Within days, we were like a married couple. We spent all of our time together.

Tracy questioned me about my background and finances. I told her my family was wealthy and lived in a chateau in France. I also told her I had a life insurance policy worth ten million dollars. When I asked about her past, she said she didn't want to talk about it because it was too sad.

Mr. Long contacted me to see how things were going. I told him, "Things are going fine, but she is a very tough woman and hard to break." I was lying. I was sure Tracy loved me.

Mr. Long said, "You need to go further. You will have to ask her to marry you." Little did Mr. Long know that I was in love with Tracy and truly wanted to marry her. I knew I should quit the case, but I couldn't. My job just didn't matter anymore.

I proposed during dinner at my place. "Tracy, I love you. Will you marry me?"

She smiled and said, "I would love to marry you."

A TURN OF EVENTS

The next week we were married in a private ceremony. We went on a luxurious three-week honeymoon to the Bahamas.

During the honeymoon, Mr. Long got in touch to remind me that this was not for real. "Don't let your emotions get the better of you. You have to remember that Tracy is a dangerous woman."

I pretended to agree, but I didn't believe him. I was in love.

After our honeymoon, Tracy said we should get our affairs in order. She asked me to make her the beneficiary of my insurance policy. I refused to be suspicious. I was sure she loved me. When I told her I had made the change, she was pleased.

One day Tracy surprised me. She said she had to go out of town on business for a few days. She was an interior decorator and had some shopping to do in London. I didn't want her to leave me, but Tracy left the next day.

I gave Mr. Long my usual check-in call. He reminded me that both of Tracy's late husbands had died while she was away from home. I didn't pay any attention to him. I was confident that she loved me more than life itself. Little did I know she was planning to make her big move.

That evening, Tracy called and said she had arrived safely. She said she missed me and couldn't wait to come back home—she missed my sexy body.

A
TERRIBLE MOMENT

After I hung up, I went to the living-room bar to get a drink. I noticed there were only two bottles of rum. I thought that was strange because we had brought several bottles back from the Bahamas.

I suddenly remembered Mr. Long reminding me to be careful about eating or drinking anything in the house. "You can't tell what she might leave for you or where it might be," he had said. I knew Tracy wouldn't do anything to hurt me, but I examined the bottles anyway. They were unopened. I poured myself a drink of rum. I relaxed on the sofa and sipped my drink.

After a few minutes, I felt dizzy and fell to the floor. I couldn't breathe. My throat was blocked. I tried to get to the phone to call an ambulance. As I touched the phone, it rang. I picked up. It was Mr. Long.

"Thank God," I whispered, "help me." He asked what had happened to me.

"I can't breathe. Send an ambulance quickly." As I put down the phone, I thought, *This is it.*

I was still awake, but I couldn't move my hands or legs. I was helpless. After a few minutes I heard banging on the door, and then the door came crashing down. It was the fire department and the paramedics.

They asked me what had happened. All I could say was, "Help me." From that moment on, I knew nothing.

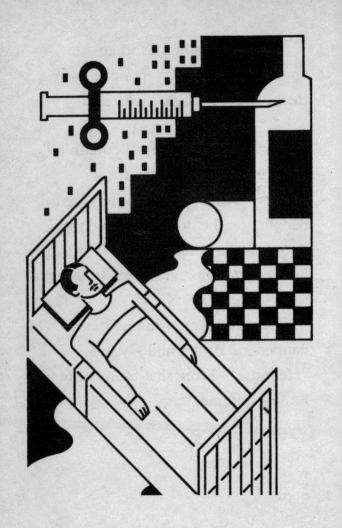

A SAD STORY

I woke up in the hospital. The first person I saw was Mr. Long. I said, "What happened to me? Why am I here?"

Mr. Long asked, "How do you feel?"

I said, "OK, I guess. What happened?"

"You were poisoned. Do you remember drinking anything?"

"I can't remember anything," I said.

He told me that the police had found a glass with traces of rum in it on the floor. "Your fingerprints were on the glass." I started to remember what had happened.

Mr. Long said, "You were in a coma for four days. Tracy is still in London. We will get her when she comes back."

I said, "How could she be responsible for this? When I opened the rum bottle, the top was still sealed." I just couldn't accept the truth.

He said, "The bottle of rum you drank from was poisoned. When the police tested the bottle in the lab, they found a tiny hole in the cap. They think Tracy pierced it with a surgical needle and shot the poison in that way. This is probably what happened to Tracy's other two husbands."

I got out of the hospital two days later. Mr. Long told me to get a hotel room and lay low. There was only one way to get Tracy to come back. "We will pretend you are dead," he said.

A TRAP IS SET

Mr. Long had the police call Tracy in London to tell her I was dead. She said, "What happened to my husband?" The policeman told her I had overdosed on alcohol. Tracy said that she would return the next day.

The next morning, Mr. Long and I prepared for her. He took me to the morgue where a make-up specialist made me look dead. In an hour, I was ready. I looked dead.

A policeman brought Tracy to identify my body. She started to cry when she saw me. I felt terrible. The policeman asked her questions like, "When did you last see your husband? Did he have any financial problems?" The policeman seemed satisfied with Tracy's answers.

Tracy asked when the police would release the body so she could make funeral arrangements. The police told her, "Whenever you want to have the funeral, we will not stand in your way." She scheduled the funeral for the following afternoon.

Mr. Long and I had a talk after

Tracy left. I was very depressed. He tried to convince me it was all part of the job. He said that he had known this day would come. I had succeeded in trapping Tracy. I had proved she was a black widow. He told me that it had been a tough assignment. I had to try to control my emotions.

That night in my hotel room, I couldn't sleep. I kept thinking about what would happen the next day — the final conflict.

THE FINAL CONFLICT

The day of the funeral was like no other. First, I called Mr. Long to ask when I should be at the funeral home to get ready. Mr. Long said the funeral was scheduled for 12:30, but we would need time to prepare.

Before I left, I opened my wallet and looked at Tracy's photo. It brought back wonderful memories. She looked so beautiful.

When 12:30 came, I was lying in my casket. I was wearing my best suit, and the make-up people had made me very pale. Mr. Long had told me to be as still as possible. I opened my eyes a crack to peek at the people in the room. Then, Tracy arrived, looking pale and sad.

She approached me in my casket and started to cry. My heart went out to her. I still loved her. I sat up and held my arms out to her.

Tracy jumped back and cried out in shock. Then a terrible expression came across her face as she realized that I was alive. She was furious to see that she had been tricked.

Tracy pulled a gun from her bag and aimed it at me. "I hate you, I've always hated you!" she screamed. All at once, everyone brought out their guns. The visitors were all undercover police officers. I ducked down in the coffin as she pulled the trigger. Guns went off all over the room. Tracy collapsed on the floor.

I couldn't help myself. I jumped out and ran over to hold her while we waited for an ambulance. "I love you," I whispered. She turned her head away and died.

Mr. Long announced, "It's over, everybody." He looked at me and said, "Back to work, Louis."

10

BACK TO BUSINESS

Mr. Long and I went with the police to Tracy's apartment the next morning. Mr. Long wanted to see if we could track down any of the insurance money.

It was the last place I wanted to be. I was in a daze and felt ill. I just couldn't believe that Tracy had betrayed me and that she was dead. But Mr. Long needed my help, and

I had to get all of my personal things out of there.

We found Tracy's passport and a plane ticket to London on the hall table. Tracy must have been planning to leave as soon as she returned from my funeral.

A policeman said, "Look, there's a message on the answering machine. Let's listen to it."

The message was from a man with an English accent. "Darling, where are you? You weren't on the plane. I've been waiting for hours to hear from you. Call me. I love you." Tracy already had her next victim lined up.

I felt terrible and had to be alone. I went into Tracy's bedroom and sat on the bed. A book on the bedside table caught my eye, and I picked it up. It was Tracy's diary. I started reading it.

What I read shocked me. Tracy's diary was full of pure hatred—hatred for all men—for me, for her other husbands and especially for her father, whom she described as a drunk who beat and abused her.

It was upsetting to read about how poor she was as a child and how she had decided to get a lot of money any way she could. And how she could never get enough money and kept craving more and more and more.

I couldn't believe that someone who had looked so beautiful and seemed to be so gentle could have been so full of poison.

Mr. Long and I left Tracy's apartment. He had found Tracy's financial records and was happy that we could recover some of the money she had falsely inherited.

As for me, it's back to business. And business and pleasure just don't mix. I'll never let another woman make a fool out of me again.

Never.

A DISCUSSION
WITH ANDRE HOLDER

by Gretchen Van Nuys

GRETCHEN: How did you decide to write this story?

ANDRE: I was at my job, and I was passing by the TV. A commercial was on for *A Kiss Before Dying*, and it made me think of writing a story like it. I think I started that night.

GRETCHEN: Did you plan to write a whole book, or did it just happen?

ANDRE: It just sort of happened.

A bunch of pieces came together, and it just continued. I originally planned a short story.

GRETCHEN: How long did the story take you to write?

ANDRE: I never timed how long it took—maybe three months. Sometimes I wrote every day, sometimes I didn't touch it for a week or two.

GRETCHEN: Did you share this with anyone while you were writing it?

ANDRE: I shared it with my tutor. I wanted to write it to surprise her, but she peeked and saw it and thought it was great.

GRETCHEN: Did you write about people you know?

ANDRE: I made up all of the characters. The names were the hardest part. I started the whole story by making up the title *Fatal Beauty* and thinking of what kind of story would go with that.

GRETCHEN: How did you decide what the characters look like?

ANDRE: For Tracy, I imagined someone who looks good but is real devious. It goes to show that things aren't always what they look like.

GRETCHEN: Did you have any help writing this?

ANDRE: Basically, it was all my creation. Sometimes my tutor spelled words for me. Later, you helped me edit the story and fill in some parts.

GRETCHEN: Do you think that writing this book has helped you with your reading and writing?

ANDRE: My reading is the same, but I enjoy writing more now. People tell me they like my story, and it makes me feel good about myself. It makes me want to write more. I've learned that when I get stuck with my writing, it helps to put it down for a while and come back to it later.

GRETCHEN: Would you like to write more books?

ANDRE: Yes, I would definitely like to. I'm different than most of the other students at my center. Most of them write personal things about themselves. I can't —I like detective stories, and I like action. I have to

write things that excite me, that get
me into the story.

TO OUR READERS

We hope to publish more books like this one. But to do that, we need writing by you, our readers. If you are enrolled in an adult basic-skills program or an ESOL program, we would like to see your writing. If you have a piece of writing you would like us to consider for a future book, please send it to us. It can be on any subject; it can be a true story, fiction, a play or poetry. We can't promise that we will publish your story, but we will give it serious consideration. We will let you know what our decision is.

Please do not send us your original manuscript. Instead, make a copy of it and send that to us, because we can't promise that we will be able to return it to you.

If you send us your writing, we will assume you are willing to let us publish it. If we decide to accept it, we will send a letter requesting your permission. So please be sure to include your name, address and phone number on the copy you send us.

We look forward to seeing your writing.

The Editors
Readers House
Literacy Volunteers of New York City
121 Avenue of the Americas
New York, NY 10013

Four series of good books for all readers:

Writers' Voices—A multicultural, whole-language series of books offering selections from some of America's finest writers, along with background information, maps, glossaries, questions and activities and many more supplementary materials. Our list of authors includes: Amy Tan * Alex Haley * Alice Walker * Rudolfo Anaya * Louise Erdrich * Oscar Hijuelos * Maxine Hong Kingston * Gloria Naylor * Anne Tyler * Tom Wolfe * Mario Puzo * Avery Corman * Judith Krantz * Larry McMurtry * Mary Higgins Clark * Stephen King * Peter Benchley * Ray Bradbury * Sidney Sheldon * Maya Angelou * Jane Goodall * Mark Mathabane * Loretta Lynn * Katherine Jackson * Carol Burnett * Kareem Abdul-Jabbar * Ted Williams * Ahmad Rashad * Abigail Van Buren * Priscilla Presley * Paul Monette * Robert Fulghum * Bill Cosby * Lucille Clifton * Robert Bly * Robert Frost * Nikki Giovanni * Langston Hughes * Joy Harjo * Edna St. Vincent Millay * William Carlos Williams * Terrence McNally * Jules Feiffer * Alfred Uhry * Horton Foote * Marsha Norman * Lynne Alvarez * Lonne Elder III * ntozake shange * Neil Simon * August Wilson * Harvey Fierstein * Beth Henley * David Mamet * Arthur Miller and Spike Lee.

New Writers' Voices—A series of anthologies and individual narratives by talented new writers. Stories, poems and true-life experiences written by adult learners cover such topics as health, home and family, love, work, facing challenges, being in prison and remembering life in native countries. Many *New Writers' Voices* books contain photographs or illustrations.

Reference—A reference library for adult new readers and writers.

OurWorld—A series offering selections from works by well-known science writers, including David Attenborough, Thor Heyerdahl and Carl Sagan. Books include photographs, illustrations, related articles.

Write for our free complete catalog: Readers House/LVNYC, 121 Avenue of the Americas, New York, NY 10013